To my children Storm and Eve and to all children who love whales.

A MICHAEL NEUGEBAUER BOOK
Copyright ©1992 by Verlag Neugebauer Press, Salzburg.
The Animal Family Book Series is supervised by biologist Sybille Kalas.
Published by Picture Book Studio, Saxonville, MA.
Distributed in the United States by Simon & Schuster.
Distributed in Canada by Vanwell Publishing, St. Catharines, Ontario.
Published in UK by Picture Book Studio, Neugebauer Press Ltd., London.
Distributed in UK by Ragged Bears, Andover.
Distributed in Australia by Era Publications, Adelaide.
All rights reserved.
Printed in Italy by Grafiche AZ, Verona.
10 9 8 7 6 5 4 3 2 1

Library of Congress Cataloging in Publication Data
D'Vincent, Cynthia, 1950-
The whale family book / by Cynthia D'Vincent
p. cm. – (The Animal Family books)
Summary: Describes the activities of whales, from the calving grounds among the Hawaiian Islands to the summer feeding grounds off Alaska.
ISBN 0-88708-148-7 : $15.95
1.Whales – Juvenile literature. 2. Humpback whale – Juvenile literature. [1.Whales.] I. Title. II. Series.
QL737.C4D85   1992
599.5 – dc20   91-41145

Ask your bookseller for these other Animal Family Books:
THE GOOSE FAMILY BOOK by Sybille Kalas
THE BEAVER FAMILY BOOK by Sybille and Klaus Kalas
THE PENGUIN FAMILY BOOK by Lauritz Sømme and Sybille Kalas
THE LION FAMILY BOOK by Angelika Hofer and Gunter Ziesler
THE CHIMPANZEE FAMILY BOOK by Jane Goodall and Michael Neugebauer
THE WILD HORSE FAMILY BOOK by Sybille Kalas
THE ELEPHANT FAMILY BOOK by Oria Douglas-Hamilton
THE POLAR BEAR FAMILY BOOK by Thor Larsen and Sybille Kalas
THE LEOPARD FAMILY BOOK by Jonathan Scott

Cynthia D'Vincent

The Whale Family Book

PICTURE BOOK STUDIO

The largest part of our world is covered with water. Beneath the surface of our seas lie some of earth's tallest mountains and deepest canyons, along with some of our greatest mysteries.

Though the oceans dramatically affect our everyday lives, in many ways they are even less understood and less explored than the distant heavens. Even today, the seas harbor many creatures that have never been seen by man. Sadly, there are other ocean animals that will never be seen by man again because they have been hunted into extinction. The majestic whale came close to sharing this end, but is now coming back from the very brink of extinction.

Whales were once commercially important to man and were used in many ways. The oil rendered from the blubber made excellent fuel for oil lamps, superb lubrication for precision instruments, and a fine base for creating cosmetics. Baleen from the whales' mouth was like an early–day plastic, and was used in corsets for ladies, ribs for umbrellas, and flexible buggy whips. Ambergris from the intestines of diseased sperm whales made delightful perfume, while spermaceti from the sperm whale's head was used to make candles. In addition, whale meat was prized by the people of many countries.

By the turn of this century, men armed with harpoons were sailing from ports around the world in search of the great whales. Their work was extremely dangerous, and men lost their lives – but far more whales lost theirs. Before the commercial whaling began in the 1800's, more than 120,000 humpback whales roamed the world's oceans. By the middle of this century there were only about 10,000 humpback whales left worldwide. Other whale species also suffered greatly. The gray whale that makes the longest migration of any mammal almost disappeared, as did the right whale, so named because it was the "right" one to kill due to its thick blubber.

Since 1972 these great creatures have been protected from hunting by most nations, and slowly their numbers are increasing. Now people sail the seas to learn about the whales rather than to kill them, and as a result we are beginning to understand some of the mysteries surrounding these remarkable animals.

The large group of animals to which the whales, dolphins, and porpoises belong, is called the cetaceans, and they are all mammals. Like you and me, they breathe air, are warm blooded, are highly intelligent, and have hair or the remnants of hair.

Their babies are born alive instead of hatched from eggs, and they nurse their young from mammary glands.

Until recent years, very little has been known about these powerful leviathans. Whether feared or loved, the mysteries surrounding whales have captured the imagination of man, particularly the haunting, beautiful song of the humpback whale.

Through research some of these mysteries are being solved. While it is critical that we learn as much as we can about whales, such knowledge is still only a part of what it will take to protect them. If people continue to care as much about whales as they do now, then whales and their calves will continue to swim free in the seas to blow their peaceful blows and lift their graceful flukes.

For many years I have been sailing the seas, studying different species of whales, but mostly the humpback whale. I sail aboard our square-rigged sailing ship Varua with my husband Russ, who is the Captain, and our two children, Storm and Eve.

Ever since they were born, Storm and Eve have been sailors, living among the whales. Over the years they have watched calves grow into rambunctious juveniles, and seen familiar adults return to the same place to feed season after season. They have seen killer whales attack young humpbacks, and watched sea lions clamber off their rocks to harass whales that swim too near. They are also learning how all the animals in the sea are part of a big system, and how fragile that system really is.

The humpback whale has always fascinated me because it is the most acrobatic of all the great whales, and because it also seems to have the most complex social relationships. It averages about 50 feet in length, about the size of a school bus, and weighs about 100,000 pounds, which is as much as our sailing ship weighs.

Its long sweeping flippers, also known as pectoral fins, are almost one third as long as its body. These flippers make it different from all other whales, and they are responsible for the humpback's scientific name in Latin, Megatera novaeangliae, which means "big winged New Englander." The flippers, which are often white in color, have knobs of flesh on the leading edge. Knobs or bumps are also found on the snout, and from each one grows a single hair, the humpback's last trace of mammalian hair. The purpose of these bumps or sensory nodules is not entirely understood, but they may help the whale to detect its prey. The tail fin of a humpback is called a fluke and its trailing edge is usually scalloped. The fluke is over 15 feet long from tip to tip, which is five feet longer than a basketball hoop is high, and a few feet longer than the little boat from which I do my daily work. Unlike fish tails that are vertical and flip from side to side, the fluke is horizontal and sweeps forcefully up and down to propel the whale through the water.

Over the past 60 million years the whale has made the greatest evolutionary change of any other mammal. Though the origin of cetaceans is still uncertain, genetic studies suggest that modern day cetaceans are most closely related to hoofed animals. Fossil evidence suggests that the whale may once have roamed along the prehistoric shores as a wolf-sized animal with 5 little hoofs instead of claws on each foot. Some 50 million years ago, the land mammal moved into the sea, and these first whales were called archaeocetes, which means ancient whales. When the whale began living entirely in the water, the downward pull of gravity disappeared, and because this limitation on its size and weight was gone, the whale gradually became bigger and more power-ful than any of the other mammals it had left behind on dry ground.

So that the whale could breathe easier as it came up for air, over millions of years the nose on the front of its head became the blowhole on the top of its head; and so that it would have good steering and stability as it swam through the sea, the front arms turned into rigid flippers. The flippers of most present day whales have the same arm, wrist, and finger bones that their mam-malian ancestors had, complete with five fingers.

To become the most powerful swimmer and traveler in the sea, the hind legs diminished and the tail grew to develop the large horizontal tail flukes; and so that the whale would be streamlined, the external features, such as ears, breasts, and sex organs were hidden inside slits in the body. For protection from the cold, the hairy coat of its ancestor was exchanged for the whale's thick layer of fat, called blubber.

Whales range in size from the little 5 foot La Plata dolphin to the 100 foot blue whale, which is even larger than the largest dinosaur. The blue whale is the largest animal that has ever existed on earth. One blue whale can weigh as much as 30 elephants.

There are two distinctly different groups of whales – those that have teeth and a single blowhole, and those that have baleen and two blowholes. Dolphins and sperm whales are toothed whales, called odontecetes. The humpback and the blue whale are called mysticetes, and instead of teeth they have strange looking baleen plates. Even though the baleen is inside the whale's mouth, someone must have thought that it looked like a man's mustache, because mysticete means "mustached whale."

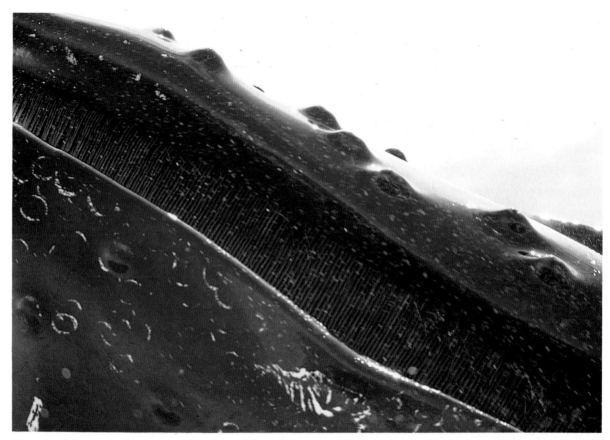

The baleen plates are arranged in a mysticete's mouth in much the same way the bristles are arranged on a broom – packed together tightly at the top and spread out or frayed at the bottom. These long strips of baleen enable the whale to strain out the very tiny animals or small fish that they feed upon.

It is interesting that some of the world's largest creatures live by feeding on some of the smallest animals in the sea. A blue whale can eat over 100 pounds of food every time it swallows – over 9,000 pounds a day. Because of this tremendously effective way of gathering and eating huge quantities of food, the mysticetes have been able to become the largest of all the cetaceans.

As we watch whales travel freely through the seas, rising to the surface to blow and lift their flukes, we wonder what they are doing in the inky depths. How deep are they diving? How long can they stay under? And where will they next come up?

When a whale rises to the surface, it immediately "blows" – it exhales so it can take a new breath of air. Early whalers believed the blow was a spout of water, but actually it is a cloud of vapor or moist "used up" air that a whale pushes out of its lungs. To a certain extent, whales can be identified by their blows. The humpback has a distinctive upside down pear-shaped blow that rises up 20 to 30 feet and hangs in the air if the day is still enough. It can be seen at great distances, and this is how whales were spotted by whalers and nearly brought to extinction in years past. Today we use the blow as an indication of a whale's activities. By counting the blows and the length of time it stays underwater, we can tell how deep it is diving. Many blows followed by a dive that lasts more than 5 minutes generally means that a whale has gone deeper than 100 feet. We can also tell how excited the whale is by the speed at which it exhales. A slow, lazy blow is often heard from a resting animal whereas a fast wheezed blow is heard from an excited animal that might be feeding heavily or perhaps has detected the presence of killer whales. Occasionally, the air is exhaled so rapidly that it sounds as if someone has blown a trumpet – a blast so loud it can be heard far across the water and will echo off any nearby mountains.

When people swim underwater for long periods, they must breathe using scuba gear, and as they breathe, a gas called nitrogen builds up in the blood. If a person comes up to the surface too quickly after a long, deep dive, this nitrogen causes a painful condition called "the bends." But whales don't breathe underwater: they hold their breaths, and their bodies use the oxygen from their lungs very efficiently, mostly for the heart and brain. This enables them to dive to great depths, and to come up very quickly without harming themselves.

Most baleen whales do not go deeper than several hundred feet because their prey lives fairly near the surface. Still, some baleen whales have been known to dive as deep as 1,500 feet. The toothed whales, in particular the sperm whales which feed on giant squid, are known for much deeper dives. A sperm whale was found entangled in cables on the ocean's floor at 3,720 feet, and scientists believe that these giant cetaceans can dive as deep as 10,000 feet. Sperm whales have been known to stay underwater for over an hour, and we often see humpbacks stay down for 10 to 15 minutes. Whales sometimes travel great distances underwater on one breath, and it is often difficult to predict where they will come up next. This is one of the most exciting and sometimes frustrating sides of whale research. When they do surface after a long dive, they push out a tremendous blow, with air rushing out the blowhole at almost 300 miles per hour.

Every year Pacific humpbacks travel some 5,000 miles as they migrate between the cold waters of Alaska and the warm waters of the tropics. The northern waters are the feeding grounds, and the tropics are the calving grounds.

While the snow flies in Alaska, males court and mate with females in the warm southern waters, and the pregnant females give birth to their babies. The males are called bulls, the females are called cows, and the babies are called calves. When observing during winter in the tropics, we often see three-somes of whales: a mother, her year-old calf, and a male escort. The male will violently defend his position in the threesome against other males, and we have seen whales with bleeding nodules on their snouts from the tail slaps of a competing male.

The sharp barnacles on the tails and the tips of the flippers make dangerous weapons, and sometimes a defending male will even try to block the blowhole of an intruder to discourage him from further pursuit.

The beautiful song of the humpback whale is sung on the calving grounds. It is believed that only the males sing, and while nobody is certain of the song's purpose, it's thought to be a courting song, perhaps indicating that the lone male singer is available or ready to mate. As we lie in our bunks at night and listen to the eerie melody seeping through the hull, it's easy to understand why in olden times, sailors thought the song came from the lips of a lovely mermaid – rather than from a 50 ton sea creature with bumps on his head.

Most Pacific humpback whales spend the winter in the waters surrounding the Hawaiian Islands, though some travel to Mexico and others to islands south of Japan. The beautiful volcanic islands of Hawaii are surrounded by reefs, and the warm waters are studded with many shallow bays and channels. These protected waters are ideal for a mother whale who is looking for a safe place to have her baby.

A female generally gives birth every two to three years to a single calf. The calf, born tail first, sometimes needs to be pushed to the surface by its mother or another whale for its first breath of air. At birth it weighs about 2 tons and is some 16 feet in length. It will grow very quickly as it nurses from its mother and consumes about 120 gallons of milk each day. This thick milk, similar to condensed cow's milk, is squirted three gallons at a time into the mouth of the calf within just a few seconds. Nursing on such rich milk makes the calf gain weight quickly.

By March, most of the whales have begun their journey back to the cold waters of the North.

The calves and their mothers are the last to leave the protected island waters, because the calves need to gain every bit of strength they can before the long journey north.

How are the whales able to find their way over so many thousands of miles to the same part of Alaska where they come year after year, or back again to the Hawaiian Islands, which are not much more than dots in the wide Pacific Ocean?

Nobody really knows, but some say they use the stars or sun to navigate, and even refer to the land masses they can see when they rise up in a spyhop to look about.

Others say that iron deposits in the frontal lobes of their brains allow them to follow the earth's magnetic field like a gigantic map. To further complicate the theories, it is interesting that some whales do not return to the places where they were born, as salmon do, but can go to Hawaii one winter and Mexico the next.

Almost all of the Pacific humpback whales go to Alaska for the summer to feed in the cold rich waters of the north. The long days and cold waters make ideal conditions for the plankton to bloom profusely. Thousands of birds return here each year to feed upon the fish that feed upon the plankton.

Salmon return to migrate up the streams to where they were spawned, and bears roam the shores to snare the struggling salmon in their claws. Mountain goats perch on craggy cliffs, and below, harbor seals haul themselves out of the water to lie on icebergs and warm themselves in the sun. Alaska is a land of such remarkable beauty that they say if once you visit here, a little bit of you will remain and keep calling you back. So it is with my family and I aboard Varua as we return each year with the whales.

By the time the whale family reaches Alaska the calf will weigh about 15 tons. Though the calf will continue to nurse throughout the first year, once they get to Alaska we often see these youngest calves alongside their mothers, feeding on herring or krill.

As with all animals in the wild, the calf must learn very quickly how to fend for itself. It soon begins to breach or slap its tail or flipper on the water, and this helps develop its coordination and muscles while preparing its defenses. Calves are full of curiosity and playfulness.Though they are closely guarded by their mothers in the early months, once in Alaska, calves will spend hours alone–playing with a piece of kelp, doing their frisky aerial antics, and other- wise entertaining themselves–while their mothers devote full attention to feeding.

The tongue then forces the water out between the 260 to 400 baleen plates which hang from the upper jaw. The baleen acts like a sieve, and thousands of tiny creatures are trapped in the whale's mouth to be swallowed after the water is pushed out.

The throat itself is very small, so humpbacks cannot swallow anything much bigger than a baseball.

While on the feeding grounds, the humpbacks spend most of their time eating, day and night, for they must consume a full year's supply of food during the three or four months they spend in Alaska.

Krill avoid bright light, so during the day the whale spends much of its time diving into the darker water below 100 feet. It surfaces only to blow several times, and then lifts its flukes to dive right back down again. In the morning or evening, or on cloudy days when there is less light, the whale changes its

feeding technique to feed on the krill that have come closer to the surface. It may roll on its side in a lateral lunge and glide fifty feet or more through patches of krill on the surface. Sometimes two or three whales will line up in a row and roll onto their sides to feed one right after another so the prey that escapes one whale's mouth will fall into the next one's. We have seen as many as eight whales lunging through the prey, lined up like dominoes. This is called echelon feeding.

A very rare feeding behavior we have seen only a few times is called flick feeding. We usually see it when there is a lot of wind and low light so that the krill is near the surface. To concentrate the krill, the whale flicks its tail towards its head, which creates a wave that rolls right over the whale towards its mouth. It then surfaces through the krill, filling its mouth with the tiny creatures.

We have seen a whale use a spyhop to get his food. The whale turned vertically in the water so that it came straight up, and as it sank back down, a whirlpool was created which must have concentrated the krill. The whale immediately came up through the swirl with its mouth open, engulfing the prey.

One of the humpback's most ingenious feeding techniques is the bubble net. A whale or a group of whales will dive down below the prey, and blow a circle of bubbles that expand as they rise. These bubbles act like a rising net. Both fish and krill can be trapped by these nets, and with the surface of the water above and the whale below, the prey has no escape.

Perhaps the greatest spectacle in the entire animal kingdom happens when a number of humpbacks come together to feed cooperatively on schools of fish. Small fish such as herring are very high in calories which the whales need, but they are also much faster and more agile than the big humpbacks.

When the whales group together they can outmaneuver and surround the herring. They create bubble nets around a school of fish, and the bigger the net, the more fish are trapped, and the more whales can feed. When they cooperate they sing a feeding song, which only lasts about a minute. This intense sound probably frightens the herring, causing the school to go into a tight ball.

This ball formation is a good protective response against predators such as salmon which catch individual fish, but it doesn't work well at all when the predators are so large that a group of them can consume almost the entire school in a series of single gulps.

The ring of bubbles traps thousands of herring. As the fish rush to the surface in a last desperate attempt to escape the net and the whales below, the song stops.

The whales burst through the surface like monsters from the deep with their mouths agape, each one with almost enough room to park a small car, and each one full of the little silver herring.

When we watch this feast of the whales, it appears that there is order to this feeding frenzy, and that the whales are maintaining a specific formation each time they surface. What looks like chaos is really more like a carefully choreographed ballet.

Though the humpbacks are primarily intent on feeding when in Alaska, remember they are one of the most acrobatic of the great whales, and they will take time out now and then to perform their spectacular aerial behaviors.

Occasionally a whale will breach and when it does it must launch some 50 tons out of the water, which comes crashing back down with unbelievable force. I have had whales breach so close to me that had they fallen in the wrong direction, I would have been crushed. But they seem to have a degree of control over their bodies, for we have seen two and even three whales breach in perfect synchrony.

They even tend to avoid landing on their stomachs so the delicate organs in that area will not be crushed as they land. What would make a whale expend that much energy? Breaching is certainly dramatic, and it may be a way that the whales express themselves, or there may be other causes. Often when the wind picks up and seas become choppy, the whales begin to breach.

Perhaps they breach to knock off parasites. Whales will sometimes breach when surprised, and I know of kayaks that have been crushed by startled whales. Another occasion when a whale may breach is when it leaves a group. Perhaps it announces its departure this way, or perhaps it is expressing anger because it has been rejected by the group.

Each day I launch my little boat from Varua so that I can silently observe the whales. Through recordings of their songs we can learn more about the feeding groups, how songs affect their prey and how the songs vary between groups. Through pictures of their tails we can tell individual whales apart, for each whale's tail is unique, like a human's thumbprint. Knowing individuals helps us see patterns in their behavior, and such knowledge helps us notice changes and then look for the reasons why the changes are occurring.

One day near nightfall after I had been working many hours in my little boat, I packed up my equipment and prepared to return to Varua. About a half mile away a group of humpbacks moved slowly toward me, blowing tall golden blows that hung in the air as the whales foraged for herring. One by one the whales began to fluke up and disappear into the depths. As I sat contemplating the whales and packing up my equipment, I began to hear the feeding song – without the aid of my hydrophone! I knew that whales had travelled very far while underwater and had come into a school of herring quite close to my little boat, for the song was growing louder and louder. All the herring around me stopped their surface swimming as they dove for safety, and aside from the eerie song, a fearsome silence fell upon the evening.

I wanted to move my boat but didn't know which way to go, so I decided to stay right where I was. This time I could see no bubbles to warn me where the whales would come up, so I quickly scanned the water for any sign, and even looked over the side of my boat.

As I stared intently into the water, I suddenly saw the white flash of flippers on every side of me and the silver flash of herring as they fled to the surface. 900,000 pounds of whales surrounded my little 300 pound boat as the whales blasted through the water with such force that I felt as if I were in a whirlpool. Huge jaws wrapped around my boat and dripping baleen hung above me. At that moment I think I must have felt as Jonah did as he was swallowed by a whale. But these whales didn't want to swallow me or even harm me, and they quickly slid back into the water.

All that remained were a few terrified herring lying in the bottom of my boat and the reflection of the snowcapped mountains on the perfectly calm water. Within minutes the whales were lunging elsewhere, apparently undisturbed by what had happened.

That evening as Varua gently rocked at anchor. I sat on deck with my family and talked about the day. We could hear the gentle whoosh of whales blowing nearby as we watched the glorious colors of the northern lights play across the Alaska sky. As the whales lifted their graceful flukes to dive, the golden rays of the setting sun turned the droplets of water from their tails into beautiful prisms. From beneath the glassy sea we could faintly hear their haunting song.

This day had been very exciting, and while some days are more memorable than others, every day makes us feel that it is a great privilege to share the earth with these extraordinary animals – and we are thankful that the magnificent whale has survived.